Mother Goose's Little Misfortunes

MOTHER GOOSE'S LITTLE MISFORTUNES

SELECTED BY

Leonard S. Marcus and Amy Schwartz

ILLUSTRATED BY

Amy Schwartz

Bradbury Press   New York

Several sources were invaluable to me in preparing this book's
introduction. They include: *The Oxford Dictionary of Nursery Rhymes*
edited by Iona and Peter Opie; *The Annotated Mother Goose* edited by
William S. Baring-Gould and Ceil Baring-Gould; *Mother Goose's
Melodies* edited by E. F. Bleiler; X. J. Kennedy's "Disorder and
Security in Nonsense Verse for Children," in *The Lion and the
Unicorn,* Vol. 13, No. 2; and my interview with Iona Opie in the
same issue of *The Lion and the Unicorn.*

— L.S.M.

Bradbury Press
An Affiliate of Macmillan, Inc.
866 Third Avenue, New York NY 10022
Collier Macmillan Canada, Inc.

The text of this book is set in Goudy Old Style.
The illustrations are rendered in watercolor.
Book design by Amy Schwartz
Typography by Julie Quan
Printed and bound in Hong Kong
First American Edition
10   9   8   7   6   5   4   3   2   1

LIBRARY OF CONGRESS CATALOGING-IN-PUBLICATION DATA
Mother Goose. Selections.
Mother Goose's little misfortunes / selected by Leonard S. Marcus and Amy Schwartz ;
illustrated by Amy Schwartz.
p.   cm.
Summary: A collection of Mother Goose nursery rhymes dealing with
misfortunes of various kinds.
ISBN 0-02-781431-9
1. Nursery rhymes.   2. Children's poetry.   [1. Nursery rhymes.]
I. Marcus, Leonard S., date. II. Schwartz, Amy. III. Title.
PZ8.3.M85   1990
398.8 — dc20   89-77425   CIP   AC

For Terri,

Claudia,

&

Chris

Mother Goose rhymes, as every reader of them is bound to know, often deal with unsettling matters — the prospect of being devoured whole, among others:

> Jerry Hall
> He is so small,
> A rat could eat him
> Hat and all.

Farfetched and wondrously concise, it's their curious triumph to turn outrageous misfortune into cunning verbal toys, allowing us, young and old, to view our worst fears and wildest imaginings from a safe remove. Standing back, it becomes possible for us to have a good laugh over types of experience that might otherwise, as literally happens to the unfortunate Anna Elise, set one spinning.

Every four- and forty-year-old has known the indecision that stymies the robin and the robin's son, felt as perilously small as we're told Jerry Hall is, and gone round in circles of panic like Poor Dog Bright and Poor Cat Fright. Everyone has wanted to say, "Off goes his head!" and be done with some loathsome person, or at any rate to tell some such person off with the admirable candor of the rhyme that begins: "I do not like thee, Doctor Fell."

Figures of authority like Fell and Corporal Tim are routinely upended in the rhymes, a reversal of the usual order that the young, who are also by and large the powerless, can readily appreciate. And just as there are also times when what children want above all is to be treated exactly like their elders, so too there are Mother Goose rhymes in which the young are not automatically let off lightly. Little Miss Tuckett may get to enjoy her bowl of peaches and cream but, as everyone knows, Little Miss Muffet was, and will forever remain, less fortunate.

To notice only the content of the poems, though, is to miss a good portion of what they're about. The buoyant rhythms and rhymes of the verses set them off as inherently playful material. It's a clue to their real nature that Mother Goose rhymes, regardless of their subject matter, are such fun to say aloud:

> Here lies old Fred.
> It's a pity he's dead…
>
> Rain, rain, go to Spain,
> Never show your face again.

Some verses have specific play-associations as well. "He loves me./ He don't..." is a fortune-telling rhyme that children have skipped to. The rhyme about the "old woman called Nothing-at-all" may have started out as a riddle, though we no longer remember its answer.

As Walter de la Mare observed, many Mother Goose rhymes are also "tiny masterpieces of word craftsmanship." In the verses about Jerry Hall and Gotham's wise men, the very brevity of the poems speaks volumes about their subjects' extreme predicaments. The poem about the monkey who "When he/Fell down/Then down/Fell he" teases by slyly taking the form of an explanation of woe, but without supplying the comforting substance of one. The high-toned manner of the rhyme that begins: "Alas! Alas! for Miss Mackay!" is completely — and thus comically — at odds with the sheer chaos of the heroine's dilemma.

In striking contrast to the freewheeling disorder that the poems frequently evoke is the equally extreme orderliness of the verses themselves, with their regular rhyme schemes and inescapable rhythms. X. J. Kennedy has aptly compared the strict form of such poems to a "safety net" that reassures young readers as they explore an otherwise wide-open imaginative terrain where wishes and fears alike have free rein and seemingly anything can happen.

Virtually all Mother Goose rhymes are of unknown authorship. Most persons mentioned in them are, like Mother Goose herself, wholly imaginary. One notable exception to the latter rule is John Fell (1625–86), Dean of Christ Church, Oxford — the same university college where two centuries later the Reverend Charles Dodgson taught mathematics and, as Lewis Carroll, gained nonsense immortality as the author of the "Alice" books.

The real Dr. Fell, it is said, offered a student facing expulsion a chance to redeem himself by translating extemporaneously a certain verse from the Latin. The student's free rendering, into which he rather brashly introduced the dean's own name, is the Mother Goose rhyme about unutterable dislike we know today. Realizing he'd been outwitted, Fell, who was feared as a strict disciplinarian, let the student stay on.

It is thus that Mother Goose rhymes disarm the killjoy and remind us all of the supreme virtue of being able to laugh at oneself. Great in spirit and nutshell small, the rhymes recast misfortune so that it looms less large. Nonsense is only partly what they're about; by a delightful paradox, their nonsense restores our sense of proportion.

— Leonard S. Marcus

Peter White will ne'er go right;
Would you know the reason why?
He follows his nose wherever he goes,
And that stands all awry.

Alas! Alas! for Miss Mackay!
Her knives and forks have run away,
And when the cups and spoons are going,
She's sure there is no way of knowing.

A robin and a robin's son
Once went to town to buy a bun.
They couldn't decide on plum or plain,
And so they went back home again.

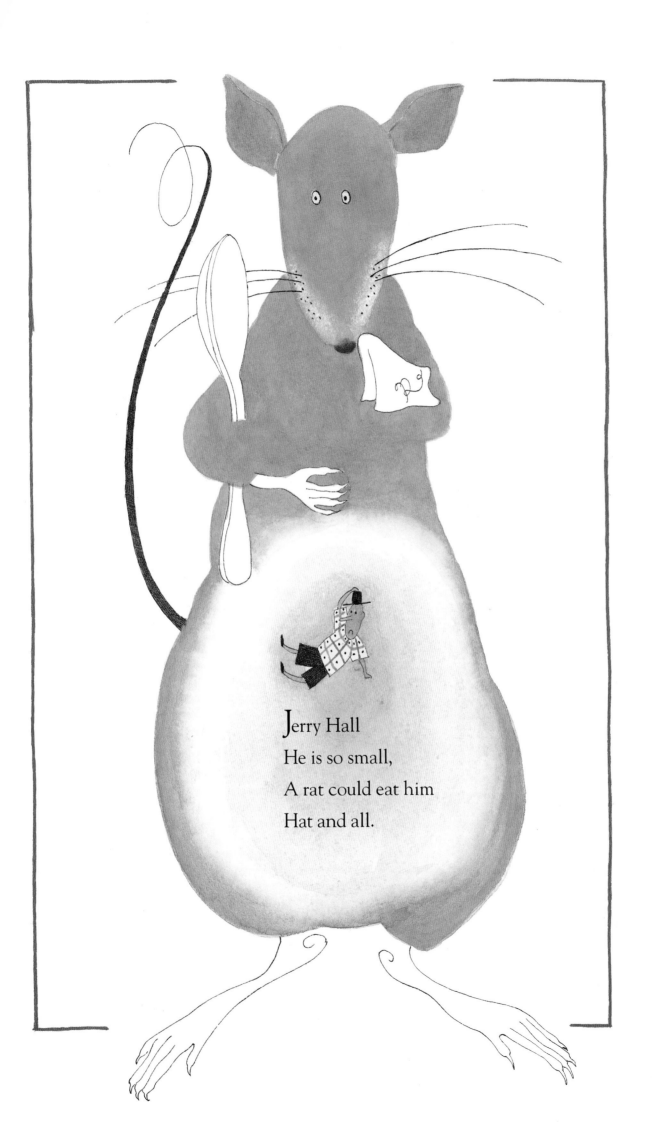

Jerry Hall
He is so small,
A rat could eat him
Hat and all.

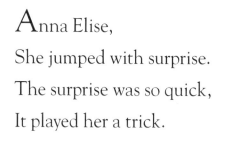

Anna Elise,
She jumped with surprise.
The surprise was so quick,
It played her a trick.

The trick was so rare,
She jumped in a chair.

The chair was so frail,
She jumped in a pail.

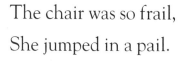

The pail was so wet,
She jumped in a net.

The net was so small,
She jumped on a ball.

The ball was so round,
She jumped on the ground.

And ever since then
She's been turning around.

Little head,
Little wit.
Big head,
Not a bit.

Here lies old Fred.
It's a pity he's dead.
We would have rather
It had been his father.
Had it been his sister,
We would not have missed her.
If the whole generation,
So much better for the nation.
But since it's only Fred,
Who was alive and is dead,
There's no more to be said.

There once were two cats of Kilkenny,
Each thought there was one cat too many.
So they fought and they fit,
And they scratched and they bit,
Till, excepting their nails
And the tips of their tails,
Instead of two cats, there weren't any.

I do not like thee, Doctor Fell.
The reason why I cannot tell.
But this I know, and know full well,
I do not like thee, Doctor Fell.

Little Miss Tuckett
Sat on a bucket,
Eating some peaches and cream.
There came a grasshopper,
And tried hard to stop her,
But she said,
"Go away, or I'll scream!"

There was
A monkey
Climbed
A tree.

When he
Fell down,
Then down
Fell he.

Poor Dog Bright
Ran off with all his might,
Because the cat was after him,
Poor Dog Bright!

Poor Cat Fright
Ran off with all her might,
Because the dog was after her,
Poor Cat Fright!

Corporal Tim
Was dressed so trim,
He thought them all afraid of him.
But sad to say,
The very first day,
He had a fight,
He died of fright,
And that was the end of Corporal Tim.

Fee, fie, fum,
I smell the blood
Of an earthly man.
Let him be alive or dead,
Off goes his head!

There was an old woman
Called Nothing-at-all,
Who lived in a dwelling
Exceedingly small.
A man stretched his mouth
To its utmost extent,
And down at one gulp
House and old woman went.

He loves me.
He don't!
He'll have me.
He won't!
He would if he could.
But he can't,
So he don't.

Rain, rain, go away,
Come again another day.

Rain, rain, go to Spain,
Never show your face again.

Rain, rain, go to Germany,
And remain there permanently.

Three wise men of Gotham,
They went to sea in a bowl.
And if the bowl had been stronger,
My song had been longer.

The End